ONLY NINE CHAIRS
A TALL TALE FOR PASSOVER

by
Deborah Uchill Miller
Illustrated by
Karen Ostrove

KAR-BEN COPIES, INC.   ROCKVILLE, MD.

Library of Congress Cataloging in Publication Data

Miller, Deborah.
  Only nine chairs.

  Summary: Speculates in rhyme how to handle nineteen guests at a Seder
dinner when there are only nine chairs.
  [1. Seder—Fiction. 2. Stories in rhyme] I. Ostrove, Karen, ill. II. Title.
PZ8.3.M61325On   1982   [E]   82-80035
ISBN 0-930494-12-1
ISBN 0-930494-13-X (pbk.)

Second Printing, 1983.

Published by KAR-BEN COPIES, Inc., Rockville, MD
Printed in the United States of America.

for
Arielle and Adinah
Elliot, Philip and Naomi
with special thanks to
Miriam and Naomi

At our Seder tonight
Nineteen guests are expected.

No uncles forgotten,
No cousins neglected.

That makes 19 noses
And 38 thumbs and
A whole lot of freckles
If everyone comes.

We've plenty of silverware,
Glasses and dishes,
Enough food for seconds,
The house smells delicious.

For all of these guests
We have seating for nine.
Will some have to stand
While the others recline?

We have lots of room,
But not enough chairs.
Could some sit in the attic,
Or on bookshelves in pairs?

Can they sit in the sink
Soaking suds with the pans?
Camp out in the carport
In empty trash cans?

Should they sit on the ledges?
Line up on the stairs?

We have nineteen people
And only nine chairs.

For Kiddush we stand,
That's not a chore.

But when we sit down,
Half land on the floor.

But that isn't right!
No, it just isn't fair!

I've got an idea...
Let's all sit on one chair.

We read the Haggadah,
Sing songs filled with hope,
With one book at the bottom
And a long periscope.

When it comes time to wash,
Aunt Tillie can pour.
We'll hold out our hands.
(We need drains in the floor.)

Parsley is next.
Here's how we dip it—
We lower our fishing rods...

Try not to drip it!

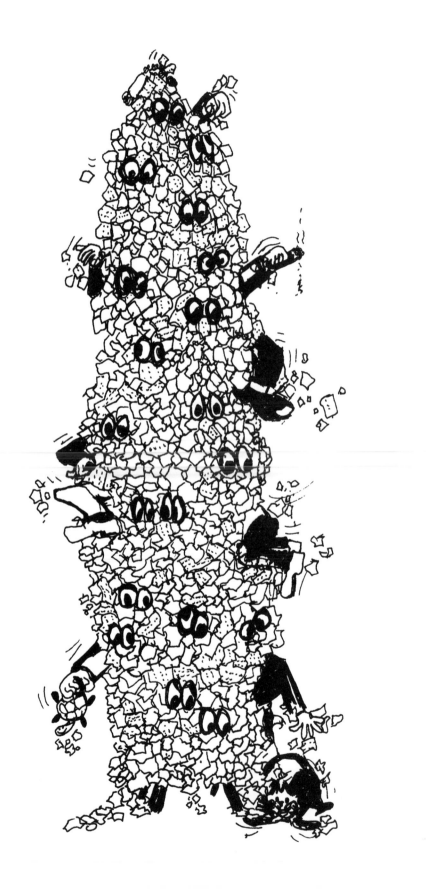

The night's filled with matzah,
We break it and hide it.
As crumbs pile up
We are hidden inside it.

It sure won't be easy
In all this congestion,
To locate the youngest
To ask the first question.

Each time we drink,

We recline to one side.

It's a hazard to us,

But we do it with pride.

Now it's time for the meal,
I have good news for you...
Climb down, everyone,
We'll share chairs two by two!

While the lefties are eating,
The righties will drink.
We'll switch in the middle,
That's fair, don't you think?

The eating is over,
The blessings recited.
We've almost forgotten
A guest we've invited.

So open the door,
Elijah is there.
And what do you know...

He brought his own chair!